As members of the
MAGIC ATTIC CLUB,
we promise to
be best friends,
share all of our adventures in the attic,
use our imaginations,
have lots of fun together,
and remember—the real magic is in us.

Alison   *Keisha*

Heather   *Megan*

Contents

Chapter 1

A New Neighbor

7

Chapter 2

Found in the Snow

15

Chapter 3

An Invitation

23

Chapter 4

Secrets in the Attic

33

THE SECRET OF THE ATTIC
by Sheri Cooper Sinykin

Illustrations by
Ed Tadiello

Spot Illustrations by
Rich Grote

MAGIC ATTIC PRESS

Published by Magic Attic Press.

Copyright ©1995 by MAGIC ATTIC PRESS

For more information contact:
Book Editor, Magic Attic Press, 866 Spring Street,
P.O. Box 9722, Portland, ME 04104-5022.

First Edition
Printed in the United States of America
5 6 7 8 9 10

Betsy Gould, Publisher
Marva Martin, Art Director
Robin Haywood, Managing Editor

Edited by Judit Bodnar
Designed by Susi Oberhelman

ISBN 1-57513-001-7

Magic Attic Club books are printed on acid-free, recycled paper.

Chapter 5

Welcome, Strangers
41

Chapter 6

A Girl Named Ellie
49

Chapter 7

The Gift
57

Chapter 8

The Magic Attic Club
65

Chapter One

A NEW
NEIGHBOR

I thought the girls invited you to go sledding."

Heather started at the sound of her mother's voice, she was so absorbed in what was going on across the street. "They did," she said, "and to their Christmas party, too. I'm supposed to bring an ornament."

"Oh." Mrs. Hardin nodded knowingly as she peeled tape from a packing box that had been stored in the basement since the family's move back to her hometown three months ago. "You want me to help you make one?" she asked.

Heather shook her head. "That's okay. Maybe I'll just stay here." She cast a wistful glance out the window at the three girls pitching snowballs in Alison McCann's front yard. Would they understand if she only went sledding with them and not to the party? What if they thought she was stuck up and didn't want to be their friend?

Heather's gaze wandered to the moving van parked at the deserted Victorian house next to the McCanns'. The girls seemed to be having too much fun even to notice it. Heather couldn't help but notice, though. Her father was a pilot and had been transferred often by his airline; Heather felt as if she'd spent her whole life packing and unpacking. Of course she'd wonder who was moving in. Maybe now she'd no longer be the new kid on the block.

Mrs. Hardin smiled. "So why don't you go join your friends? At least go sledding. It'll be fun."

Heather's breath formed steamy clouds on the chilly windowpane. Fun. That was all Alison, Keisha, and Megan had talked about before school let out for vacation—the first snowfall, going sledding and caroling, trimming the tree . . .

Heather took a deep breath and grabbed her parka. Pulling her long dark hair from under her collar, she dashed out the door.

As Alison formed another perfect ball of snow, she glanced up in time to see the Hardins' glass storm door clap shut across the street. She'd seen Heather's father out shoveling their walk early that morning, but already a fluffy white blanket had settled over it. Now Heather's white hightops all but disappeared, leaving only the holes of her footprints in the snow as the girls' newest friend hurried toward them and crossed the street.

"Hi, Keish, Megan, Ali!" Heather waved.

"Don't move!" Alison commanded, brushing snowflakes off her eyelashes and blond bangs. Taking careful aim, she expertly fired off a snowball that exploded at Heather's feet. "See that? I'm ready to pitch for the Eagles, don't you think?" She'd told the girls a zillion times she'd been dying to qualify for the team ever since her older brother had first gotten his uniform. In a couple more years, she could have as many trophies for basketball and softball and soccer as Mark had when he was twelve. "So . . . ?

So?" she prodded. "What do you think?"

"Aw, just a lucky shot," Heather teased.

"No way!" Alison laughed and packed another snowball.

Megan and Keisha gathered close to watch their longtime friend show off her throwing arm. They took up a rhythmic chant. "Go, Ali! Go, Ali! Go, Ali!"

Alison played to her audience. "Bet I can hit the tip of the V on that moving van," she boasted.

"No, don't." Megan Ryder twirled a lock of strawberry-blond hair around her finger. "Look. They're putting up the ramp. Even you could miss and hit one of the movers."

Keisha Vance tilted her head, her long dark-brown hair creeping out from beneath her purple cap as she eyed the van. How could the movers be done already? Didn't the new people have any furniture? And where were they, anyway? When the Vances moved here, her mother and father were around the whole time, making sure the movers didn't break anything.

Keisha was only five then, but she still remembered how scared she was when her mother finished nursing school and found a job in a new state. They'd been lucky that her father was hired as a hospital administrator here, too. Even so, Keisha had worried about finding her way home from school, about leaving her friends behind and making new ones. Now, though, it felt as if she'd known Megan and Alison all her life. And Heather seemed to be fitting right in with the group.

The van rumbled to a start and rolled away. Alison lobbed her missile high and long, to the exact middle of the wide depression where its tailgate had rested in the snow. "See?" She grinned smugly. "I told you."

Megan applauded politely, while Keisha made a grand gesture of doffing her ski cap and bowing low, even as she winked at Heather. "And now," said Keisha, her voice rising like an announcer's, "get we to the hillery."

Heather and Megan laughed, but Alison's lips formed a lopsided frown. "It's a Shakespeare joke," Megan explained. "You know, a takeoff on 'Get thee to a nunnery,' from *Hamlet*. Mom rented the video—not that I couldn't read it, if I wanted to."

Keisha grabbed a small, stiff plastic shopping bag from the porch and handed a larger one to Alison. "Come on, you guys. Let's get on with the fun!"

"Want to race?" asked Alison.

Megan shook her head, though her steps were brisk. She wished she were heading for the ski slopes instead. She'd fly down the mountain faster than a hawk, faster than the jet that was taking her father to the Middle East to cover another news story. Her dad had said he just couldn't turn this assignment over to anyone else. To Megan, that only meant he'd be unable to take her to his house this Christmas. The other girls would be with both their parents, as they were every day. . . .

"Megan!" Keisha called. "Come on! You, too, Heather!"

Megan sped up again and soon caught Keisha and Alison. Heather, however, lagged behind, kicking at snowdrifts, listening to the bags crackling in the cold. She wondered what sorts of ornaments were nestled inside.

As the three girls came to the old Victorian house next to the McCanns', a shimmering like butterflies' wings caught Alison's eye. Nudging the others, she pointed to a woman wearing a flowing gold neck scarf and long white coat. She was fastening a multicolored wreath to the

front door. Alison wondered what it was made of. Not evergreens, that was for sure. A thick silvery braid hung down the woman's back.

A moment later, Heather, too, looked toward the porch. The woman was opening a stepladder and clambering up. In her hand was a sign that read LESSONS. The intricately carved cornice on the old house seemed to set the new neighbor off perfectly, like the frame for a museum masterpiece. Heather couldn't help being curious.

Chapter TWO

FOUND
IN THE SNOW

ome on, you guys," Keisha called from the far
edge of the property.

But the ladder had begun to wobble beneath the
woman's feet, and Heather rushed along the perfectly
shoveled walk and up the white-painted steps. "Here, let
me help you," she said, reaching out to steady the ladder.

"Why, thank you!" The woman looked down at
Heather. Her eyes were as blue as the heart of a flame.
"I'll be done in just a moment."

The fasteners for the sign seemed to be giving the woman some trouble. Alison charged up the path and took the steps two at a time. "Here, let me do that," she said.

"I think I've got it now. But I appreciate the offer," the woman replied. She climbed down and gave an approving nod at the sign, then swept her scarf over her shoulder and extended her hand. "I'm Eleanor Goodwin. And you are . . . ?"

Waving the others closer, Alison introduced herself and Heather. "That's Keisha Vance, Ms. Goodwin," she added. "And this is Megan Ryder. We're best friends, all four of us. We go everywhere together. Well, almost everywhere."

"I'm very glad to meet you," said Ms. Goodwin.

Keisha came to the foot of the porch and pointed at the LESSONS sign. "I'd love to take lessons. What kind do you give? Acting and stuff? Voice? Dancing?" Ms. Goodwin's amused smile reminded Keisha of the Mona Lisa's. She and the others had seen a picture of the famous painting in one of Mrs. Hardin's art books and loved the way the portrait's eyes seemed to follow them.

"Precisely," said the silver-haired woman, still smiling. "All of the above, and piano, too."

"Wow!" Alison elbowed Megan. "Pretty cool, huh?"

"I'll have to tell Mom," said Megan. "She promised that

if she found a good teacher, I could start piano this year."

"Well, here I am." Ms. Goodwin smiled as she added, "And Julia Wyndham should know whether I'm good or not."

Megan's green eyes went wide. "My mom took lessons from you?"

Ms. Goodwin nodded. "Lessons . . . yes. And she wasn't the only one." She shivered abruptly, then wrapped her woolen coat close about her. "Would you girls like to come in and warm up with a nice pot of licorice tea?"

Alison started after Ms. Goodwin, but Megan hesitated. Heather whispered, "We don't really know her. And how did she know who your mom is, Megan?"

"Maybe because I look exactly like her when she was ten?" Megan shrugged. "I don't know, but maybe."

Keisha supposed that made sense. But Heather had a point about the girls not knowing Ms. Goodwin. Keisha remembered her parents' warnings about strangers well enough—how could she forget after hearing them so many times? With a younger brother and sister to take care of, she not only had to listen to her parents recite the rules of behavior twenty times a day, she also felt compelled to repeat them to Ronnie and Ashley. Mom and Dad meant well, she knew. They only wanted their kids to be safe. Still, did they have to act as if she couldn't remember anything?

"We were just going sledding," Keisha said to Ms. Goodwin. "Maybe we can come by later, after we've checked with our folks."

"Wise girl." Ms. Goodwin patted Keisha's shoulder and smiled warmly at each girl in turn. "You will tell your mothers Eleanor Goodwin said hello, won't you? I'm sure they'll remember." Despite the wintry chill, her voice rang like wind chimes in a summer breeze.

Alison, Keisha, and Heather glanced at one another with raised eyebrows as they turned toward the steps. "It was nice to meet you," Megan said for them all, then followed her friends to the sidewalk. When she reached the end of Ms. Goodwin's low picket fence, Alison was already lying on her back, giggling as she made a snow angel. With a whoop of delight, Megan and Heather joined her.

"Yahoo!" cried Keisha, flopping on her back, too, and spreading her arms and legs. As she put her tongue out to catch a few flakes, she wondered whether Ms. Goodwin would need someone to clear the snow from her walk later. The woman must be at least as old as Great Aunt Bess. Maybe I could do it after the party, Keisha thought.

Alison soon scrambled to her feet and dusted herself off. "Come on, girls! The hill's probably swarming with kids, and we still have to get our sleds."

Something glinted near the path, and Heather stopped.

"Yeah, come on," Megan said. "Don't worry, Heather. We have an extra." Maybe Heather didn't have her own sled yet. "But, wait! Aren't you going to wear boots or gloves or anything?"

"Oops!" Heather grinned sheepishly and hung her head in embarrassment. As she looked down, the light flashed again. It seemed to be just inches from her shoes. "There's something here," she said, bending to search the ground. Cold stung her bare hands. "Did one of you drop a charm or a . . . bracelet or something?"

First Megan, then Keisha knelt beside her, sweeping snow aside.

As Heather again slid her freezing fingers through the snow, they stumbled over something solid. Already clumsy with cold, they could barely grasp the slender shape. "Look!" she whispered through chattering teeth—then dropped the thing as someone bumped her arm.

As quick as a jackrabbit, Alison was beside her friends, scooping the shiny golden object from the snow. "Is this your diary key, Megan?" she asked.

Megan shook her head. With its lacy interlocking circles and old-fashioned shaft, it was much

fancier than any diary key she'd ever seen. "Keisha?"

"Don't look at me." Keisha shrugged one shoulder.

"Oh, well," said Alison, "finders keepers, losers weepers, I guess." She handed Heather the key, then clapped her on the back. "Go grab your stuff and let's get rolling."

"Better yet, let's get sliding," said Keisha with a laugh.

Heather pocketed the key, then turned home, rubbing her hands and blowing on her reddened fingers. When she glanced back, Alison was tapping her toe, though only lightly, and with a conspiratorial grin on her face.

Keisha was hopping up and down, flapping her arms as if she were flying toward the Hardins', and even Megan was making pushing motions in Heather's direction.

"Okay, I'm going," she said. "Just promise you'll wait for me."

"We promise," the girls chorused.

Heather turned again toward her house, but stole one last look at her friends, just to be sure. They hadn't moved an inch. But she was certain that the lacy curtain in Ms. Goodwin's front window had.

Chapter
Three

AN
INVITATION

Keisha, Megan, and Alison came bursting out of
the McCanns' house and slid down the front walk.
Megan barely retained her balance, even in her thick-
treaded snow boots.

"Hey, Heather, what took you so long?" called Alison,
though the rosy-cheeked newcomer, now fully dressed for
the season, was waiting for the girls where she'd left
them—in front of Ms. Goodwin's house.

"Well, my sister took my boots, and then . . . ,"

Heather began. But when Megan and Keisha laughed and Alison gave her the full-blown McCann smile, Heather realized that Alison had only been teasing. "Then I had to defrost my fingers," she said, and grinned. "So, what have you guys been doing?"

"Just talking to Alison's mom," replied Keisha, "and boy, was she surprised about Ms. Goodwin moving back to the neighborhood!"

"Her, too? What did she say? Tell me!"

Mrs. McCann seemed to know her next-door neighbor quite well. She asked the girls to return the key before they went sledding. Mrs. Hardin, it turned out, also knew Ms. Goodwin, and was glad Heather had met her. She, too, suspected that the golden key belonged to the music teacher and insisted that the girls give it back right away.

"Well, let's do it now," Alison suggested, "so we can get on to the real fun." The four friends trooped through the deepening snow and back onto their neighbor's porch.

As they stamped snow from their boots, Megan looked at Heather's empty hands. "Hey, where's your ornament? Don't tell me you forgot and have to go home again!"

Heather squirmed, looked at each girl in turn, then stared at her feet and replied finally, "We don't have any ornaments, okay?"

After a pause, Alison said, "Well, then, as soon as we

see if the key is Ms. Goodwin's, we can go straight to the hill." She pressed the doorbell.

While the chimes echoed, then faded into silence, the girls examined the wreath in front of them. It was made entirely of tiny cloth dolls, each no bigger than the girls' thumbs and dressed in brightly colored Central American clothing. If this was what Ms. Goodwin considered a Christmas wreath, what might she have inside her house?

Suddenly, the door swung open, revealing Ms. Goodwin. A royal blue woolen dress set off her eyes and silver hair. Before anyone could speak, a small white terrier shot through the doorway. "Monty, get back here," Ms. Goodwin called. "Monty, you . . . you . . ."

Keisha was already halfway to the street, whistling for him. At the sidewalk, she sat on her heels and held out her hand. Within a minute or so, the little fellow was licking her mitten, his tail whipping from side to side like the metronome Keisha's choir director once used. She picked him up and carried him back to the porch.

"Wow! Instant bonding." Megan smiled ruefully and rubbed Monty behind the ears. "I wish the dogs I pet-sit would obey me that way."

Alison cleared her throat. "Ms. Goodwin, we have something that we think belongs to you." She nudged Heather forward a little in her eagerness to get going.

Heather stumbled over her words. "I . . . I . . . You must have dropped this," she said, and held out the golden key.

"Why, thank you, Heather. I hadn't realized I'd even lost it. This key—you've no idea how important this is." The woman's warm smile confirmed that the girls had done a good deed in returning it.

But, somehow, Heather didn't want to just hand her the key and leave. "My . . . my mom said you'd probably need it. And she said I could ask about lessons."

Alison took the key from Heather's mittened palm, ready to turn it over and leave. But then she, too, found herself hesitating, wondering what she ought to say to Ms. Goodwin, and what she might find out if she were invited into the house.

"Yes, Alison?" Ms. Goodwin's eyes locked with the ten-year-old's own blue ones.

"Well, my mother said to find out what kind of lessons you're giving nowadays."

Ms. Goodwin flicked her scarf back. Her eyes twinkled as she took the key, almost tenderly, from Alison. Though she was slightly plump and only a few inches taller than any of the girls, something about the way she carried herself made her seem quite stately. "So, you want to know about lessons? What are you all interested in?"

"Any kind of sports," replied Alison quickly, then

added with a grin, "but I don't suppose you can teach me how to shoot three-pointers."

"Heather's the artist, just like her mom," said Keisha, "and Megan likes to write stories and plays and stuff. Me, I love to sing."

"She's a good photographer, too," Megan piped up. "You should see her bulletin board."

"Eh, *bien*. Girls of many talents. Good for you!" Ms. Goodwin stepped aside, inviting the girls in with a sweep of her hand.

Keisha had always wondered about this house that had stood empty for as long as she could remember. Monty squirmed in her arms as the girls nearly tripped one another, all trying to squeeze through the doorway at once.

Megan and Heather giggled self-consciously, but Ms. Goodwin didn't seem to notice. She simply led them across the wide entry hall, placing the key in a silver-lidded box on a table. To the right stood a pair of closed, dark wooden doors with red highlights. She motioned them into a sitting room on her left.

Megan's eyes got wide. Books of all sizes, many of them leather-bound, lined the far wall. She'd never seen so many books in one place outside of the library.

A long sofa and a pair of matching chairs, each with

legs exquisitely carved into lions' heads, sat opposite a deep fireplace in which tinder and logs waited to be kindled. Arranged atop a low credenza and suspended from the walls, framed photographs, small paintings, and a variety of unusual musical instruments ornamented the room. Keisha recognized only a couple of them—a rain stick and a bamboo pan pipe from a report she once did on South American percussion instruments. She couldn't resist turning the rain stick over. A sound like rushing water filled the room. "You guys, listen! Isn't this cool?"

Megan nodded, then turned to examine a crystal bowl full of picture postcards. They bore postmarks from such faraway places as Afghanistan and Zaire. She wondered how many Ms. Goodwin had actually visited—and how many her own father had while covering news stories abroad.

Heather spotted a framed marquee poster from the ballet *Giselle*. Drawing closer, she saw it was signed "To E. G. With love and gratitude, Rudi and Margot." "Omigosh!" Heather gasped. She'd certainly never met anyone in her old neighborhoods who knew such famous people. "Look who signed this! Nureyev and Fonteyn!"

Alison, however, was too intrigued by a glass-encased baseball that had been autographed by Babe Ruth and the rest of the New York Yankees.

The girls' enthusiasm and curiosity about her possessions seemed to please Ms. Goodwin. With each girl's discovery, a slight smile played on her lips. "Please, won't you all be seated?" she said at last. "Make yourselves at home. Or were you on your way somewhere?"

"Well, we were going sledding," Keisha replied, "and after that, we're having a tree-trimming party at Megan's."

Ms. Goodwin clapped her hands in delight. "I love tree-trimming parties! It seems only yesterday my mother was baking gingerbread and inviting friends from miles around to come celebrate."

No one knew quite what to say. Was Ms. Goodwin hoping for an invitation to their party? After an awkward moment, Alison cleared her throat. "Well, about the lessons," she began and sat herself between Megan and Heather. Though there was plenty of room for Keisha to sit, she stood beside them, her hand just touching Heather's arm.

Ms. Goodwin glanced toward the door across the hallway. "I was just meeting with some new pupils," she said. "If you don't mind, maybe we can talk about lessons in a—"

"We'd better go, then," Megan interrupted. "We can come back some other time." She sounded disappointed, though.

"Oh, there's no need for that." Ms. Goodwin waved aside her concern. "This won't take very long. And—forgive me for being so forward—I was really hoping to share something special with you."

"You were?" asked Heather, voicing the other girls' surprise.

"It's just that you all remind me so much of me, when I was your age—curious and full of possibilities. I was thinking you might enjoy poking around my attic for a bit. We used to have the most wonderful adventures there, my friends and I." Her memories seemed to bring a special flush to her cheeks.

"Adventures?" Alison echoed.

"Oh, definitely. Adventures and more." Ms. Goodwin grew thoughtful for a moment, then nodded as if she were agreeing with herself. "Yes, I'm sure of it. You're just the right girls to enjoy my attic. After all, you're the girls who found the key. I think you'll find it the kind of place you wish you could visit all your life." Ms. Goodwin's eyes twinkled with the telling. "Even at my age, I still feel that way."

"Well . . ." Keisha rubbed her palm with her fingertips, torn between wanting to explore and thinking they really ought to leave. Heather stared at the carpet, her face reflecting the same indecision, while Megan gazed into the fireplace.

Ms. Goodwin waited for Keisha to respond.

"I guess we could stay fifteen minutes or so," she said, taking the plunge and glancing at the others. They nodded their agreement. The decision made, the girls relaxed.

"Good. You'll need the key, then." Ms. Goodwin immediately crossed the room, opened the silver box in the entry hall, and placed the golden key on the table. "Have fun, girls. I'm sure you won't be disappointed." As she closed the paneled doors firmly, the sweet scent of vanilla sneaked out into the hall and past the faded family portraits that hung there.

"Well, Monty," Megan said, "which way do we go?" The white terrier padded off, his nails clicking on the polished wood floor. "Come on, you guys!" Retrieving the key, Megan started after him up the dimly lit staircase, her friends close behind.

Chapter

Four

SECRETS
IN THE ATTIC

The key fit only one door upstairs. Megan turned it in the filigreed brass lock. "Here goes," she said. The heavy door swung wide. A pungent smell of cedar, mixed with something sharp and biting, tumbled down the stairs to greet them.

"Whew!" Keisha waved her hand before her nose. The tension broken, the girls giggled as Megan removed the key from the lock and pocketed it.

Alison made a bugling sound. "Charge!" she cried,

rushing past the others to scramble up the wooden stairs. When the clomping and creaking stopped, a hushed "Wow!" wafted down the staircase.

"Is it dark up there?" Megan called.

"No, it's beautiful! You're not going to believe this!"

"What?" cried Keisha. "Let me see!" She took the lead.

Heather and Megan hurried after her. Before them sprawled a wide attic. A splendid oriental rug covered its plank floor. The ceiling rose at steep angles, and from its peak hung a lamp with a burgundy-and-beige floral shade. Gold fringe adorned its scalloped edge, and a satin pull-cord dangled from the center. When Megan reached up and tugged on the gold tassel, a warm, rosy glow fused with daylight from the high dormer windows.

A sturdy mahogany wardrobe stood to their left. One door hung open, revealing scarves, albums, hats, and a seemingly endless selection of clothes.

"Howdy!" drawled Alison, waving a white Stetson studded with red and blue jewels and golden stars, then perching it atop her head.

A small antique writing desk in the corner drew

Megan like a magnet. Lifting the lid, she found a tapestry-covered box and opened it. One by one she lifted out a lace sachet, a stack of letters tied with a red velvet ribbon, a packet of black-and-white photographs, and an exquisite Victorian ornament. Megan cooed with delight as she stroked the angel's porcelain face and the tiny seed pearls that nestled in its lacy gown.

Across the room, Keisha called, "Hey, check this out!"

Heather hurried to join her in front of an oak and black leather steamer trunk. The girls exchanged a silent "Shall we?" Together they reached for the latch and struggled to raise the lid. With a final heave, it opened. Clothing in a whole palette of colors seemed to bloom like flowers before their eyes.

Megan and Alison joined them, lifting garments out one by one, oohing and aahing over the spangles and flounces and lace. They had said they would go downstairs in fifteen minutes. But it would take fifteen hours to go through this trunk, to say nothing of the whole attic!

"Gee," said Megan, "where do we start?" She was sure none of them had ever seen so many different kinds of clothes—modern, practical fashions side by side with storybook styles. From ball gowns to bridal gowns, camping duds to riding breeches, there were outfits for any occasion a girl could imagine.

Heather couldn't resist touching the stiff, pink ballet tutu, while Keisha's gaze lingered on a beautiful white ball gown. A silvery ice-skating outfit caught Alison's eye, and a flowing purple gown caught Megan's.

"Start anywhere," Heather said at last. "Time's a-wasting." Snatching up a pair of shiny pink toe shoes, she sat, pulled her snow pants up to her knees, and kicked her boots off. She couldn't help laughing at her own efforts as she struggled to stuff her feet into the shoes and tie the satin ribbon around her thick socks.

"Don't keel over or anything, you guys," said Alison, with a grin, "but I think even I might learn to like dresses." She held up a blue velvet one trimmed in black, then twirled a matching beret on one finger. "See? Just the

color of my eyes, don't you think? And if I spilled something, it wouldn't even show."

"Try it on," Heather urged her.

Megan stopped fiddling with the tiny buttons on a satin gown. "I don't know, they're not ours. . . ."

"Megan," Alison spoke with exaggerated patience, "who would send four girls up to an attic on their own and not expect them to play with what they find?"

"That would hardly make any sense," Heather agreed. A golden tiara gleamed on her head and a jeweled evening bag dangled from her wrist. "But then, neither would wearing toe shoes over these socks, much less trying to stand on them. Ow!" She teetered for a moment between Keisha and Megan, then crashed to her backside on a pile of dresses, her arms and legs akimbo. She giggled, then broke into a loud, infectious laugh.

"Right," said Megan. "Well, then, this must be for you, Heather. It's perfect with your dark hair." She handed over an elegant pink dress with a lace collar and looked around for one to try herself. Alison offered her a black dress covered with golden stars.

"Megan, that's you, all right," said Keisha. "The star of the class!" She gave her friend two thumbs up, then reached for a dress covered with butterflies of every color.

"You really think this goes okay with strawberry-blond hair?" Megan slipped the dress on and raised one eyebrow.

"Black, my dear, goes great with anything." Keisha grinned as she arose, tried on her outfit, and twirled about. "See what I mean? Sure wish I could see myself, though."

Heather and Alison spoke together: "I saw a mirror when we came in . . . there's one right there."

Keisha and Megan looked around. In one corner stood a tall mirror in a gilt frame. The four friends hurried, their dresses rustling, to stand in front of it.

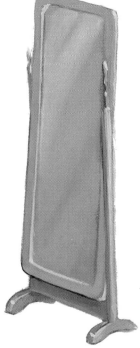

Megan whistled softly. "Hey, this looks like something right out of *Little Women*."

"Or maybe . . . Shakespeare?" Alison grinned crookedly.

Megan smiled back, then snapped her fingers. "*Little Women*! Now that's what we can play. Ali, you be Amy 'cause of your blond hair. I'll be Jo since I'm the writer and—"

"Some of us haven't read the whole book yet," said Keisha

pointedly. "And some of us don't want you to give it away."

"All right." Megan sighed. "Ali, can you see?"

"Nothing but walls and ceiling."

"I'll fix it," said Heather, reaching over and angling the mirror downward.

The four girls stepped back. Shards of light from the dormers reflected off the glass, making them all squint. Their reflections seemed to shimmer—then, all at once, to disappear.

Chapter

Five

WELCOME, STRANGERS

The girls opened their eyes. Their reflections stared back at them from the mirror—along with that of a softly lit room that not one of them had ever seen before.

"Omigosh!" gasped Heather.

"W-what happened?" Megan's voice came out in a hoarse whisper. "Where are we?"

The girls gawked at the small, cramped room. On their left was a four-poster bed covered with a flowery chintz coverlet. Just before them stood a mirror—

a tall, oblong mirror in a gilt frame. In the corner, to their right, a sturdy mahogany wardrobe hugged the wall. A steam radiator clanked and hissed beneath the window, where a fragrant pine wreath hung. A candle decoration with an incandescent "flame" glowed on the sill.

"Your guess is as good as mine," said Heather finally.

"Well, Toto," Keisha quipped, "it's for sure we're not in Kansas anymore." Megan managed a tight smile, while Alison stood stone-faced and mute.

Keisha tiptoed to the window and peered out. "Wherever we are, it's already getting dark. And look— this place is way out in the middle of nowhere!"

"How . . . how could that be?" asked Alison, moving alongside Keisha to see for herself. With a shiver, she turned away. "This is weird."

"What're we going to do?" Megan worked hard to hold her voice steady.

"I don't know, but something," said Alison. "We can't just stand here forever."

"Okay, fine. You go first, Ali." Keisha nudged her toward the door. Megan and Heather clutched each other's hands and followed close behind.

Alison poked her head out, silently beckoned the others, then ventured into the drafty hall. A strong aroma of spruce and freshly baked gingerbread meandered through the house. "It's Christmas here, at least," Alison whispered. "Come on. There must be somebody around who can tell us where we are."

Heather hurried after Alison toward the stairs, stepping lightly on the wooden floor. The click of her footsteps startled her, and she glanced down. Somehow, she was wearing party shoes. The other girls were, too. When had she changed out of the ill-fitting ballet slippers—and they out of their snow boots?

On her way downstairs, Keisha grasped the banister. It ended in a whirl of polished wood at the bottom that felt vaguely familiar. She waited for Megan and took her hand, hastening after the others down a long dark hall.

Behind closed paneled doors to their left, a Duke Ellington tune abruptly switched to a singer crooning something more Christmas-like. Keisha stared at the doors, frowned, then shook her head.

Alison, meanwhile, crossed an entry hall and found herself face-to-face with a long sofa in a modest parlor. The carved legs boasted some kind of animal face that she was quite sure she'd seen before, though the olive-

green cross-stitched upholstery was completely unfamiliar. Somehow nothing else in the room so commanded her attention—not the tall, old-fashioned radio or the fine paintings, not the scarlet, floral-bordered rug or the oval-backed chairs that flanked the fireplace.

Megan soon wandered in, pausing to glance at a folded newspaper on an end table. A headline about President Roosevelt made her pulse quicken. "You guys, I know when we are . . . kind of. Come here." As she bent to check the masthead for the city and date to confirm her guess, a door opened across the hall and a woman's voiced called out.

"Why, Heather and Keisha, I didn't know you were here! I'm sorry we kept you waiting. Come! We'll trim the tree as soon as Ellie gets here."

Alison and Megan frowned at each other, then raced to their friends' rescue.

An elegant woman with bobbed blond hair was ushering Keisha and Heather into a large living room. Though she wore a homey cardigan sweater over her straight-fitting chevron-print dress, she reminded Megan of a heroine in an old black-and-white movie. A baby grand piano between a huge Christmas tree and the fireplace caught Megan's eye.

"I sent Ellie's father after her," said the woman with a shrug. "I can't imagine what's keeping her. But you know how skating parties are." As Heather and Keisha nodded politely, the woman noticed Alison and Megan. "Oh, good. You girls are here, too." She appraised her young guests' dresses and smiled. "My, aren't those interesting frocks."

Alison had the distinct impression that what she and Heather were wearing was not the latest thing. For the life of her, though, she couldn't think how to explain. She beamed Megan a silent plea for help. Her friend was usually so good at talking to grown-ups.

"We . . . they like being old-fashioned," Megan hedged.

"Well, they're very pretty, very . . . festive." The woman glanced at the grandfather clock and sighed. "I hope Ellie's not overdoing it, her being sick so recently. The grippe hung on for weeks. But you know that, of course. Listen to me, prattling on. Where are my manners? Let me bring you some hot cider and cookies."

"We'd like that," said Keisha, hardly having to pretend at all.

As the woman's thick-heeled shoes tat-tatted down the hall, the girls clustered together, all whispering at once.

"Who is she?"

"How does she know us?"

"Who's Ellie?"

"What's the grippe?"

"The flu," answered Keisha.

"All I know," Megan whispered, "is somehow we're in the mid-thirties. The 1930s. I figured it out from a newspaper in the other room." The girls' eyes went wide.

All at once, loud thumping and banging came from the direction of the front door. Huddling close together, their pulses racing, the four friends turned toward the entryway, too stunned to run somewhere—anywhere—and hide.

Chapter Six

A GIRL
NAMED ELLIE

Within moments, the front door banged open and a man's voice called, "Come quick!"

The girls rushed into the entry hall. Megan knocked against a tall ceramic stand full of umbrellas, sending them clattering to the floor. While the others scrambled to replace them, Megan simply stared at the towering, clean-shaven man who had just come through the door. In his arms he cradled a girl about their age, bundled in an overcoat that was obviously his, since he wore only a

striped gray suit. Behind him, several boys and girls stood soberly looking on.

"Margaret! Mother!" the man called again. "Quickly, please! It's Ellie! She's had an accident!"

From the back of the house came a staccato of footfalls and cries of concern. Alison directed the others back against the wall, out of the way, to let the woman who'd greeted them earlier and an older woman pass.

"Charles, what happened?" asked his wife, reaching out to the shivering girl.

"She fell through the ice," one of the skaters piped up. "I almost did, too."

"Good heavens!" The older woman rounded up the bundled children as if they were sheep, herding them gently out the door. "Thank you for seeing Ellie home, but you'd better run along now, while we get her warmed up."

Several children spoke at once. "Will Ellie be all right?" "I could get Dr. Norman." "What about the party?"

"We'll have to call you later. Right now, we'd best see to Ellie." As the woman closed the door, she poked hairpins into the knot at the back of her neck, then pressed close to feel the drenched girl's forehead. "Take her upstairs, Charles. You two," she said, indicating Keisha and Alison, "go on up and draw a hot bath. And Margaret"—she turned to Ellie's mother—"you start heating blankets."

Her firm, no-nonsense manner reminded Heather of Grandma Hardin. "Can we do something to help?" Heather asked.

The spry woman nodded. "Come with me. We'll fix up a mustard plaster and some hot-water bottles."

Ellie's mother stroked her daughter's wet hair. "You'll be fine, darling," the woman whispered. "Don't you worry now."

Ellie's teeth stopped chattering for a moment. "Oh, Mama, I've ruined the party, haven't I? I—I'm sorry, truly I am. I didn't mean to. It was just so much fun, finally getting out. . . ." Her voice caught and the chattering resumed.

"I know, darling." Ellie's mother waved her husband upstairs and turned to the four girls. "Thank goodness you're here. We can use the extra hands."

"We'll do what we can," Keisha said, and hurried off with Alison after Ellie and her father.

The tiled bathroom was huge and drafty. A pedestal sink and a freestanding bathtub with claw feet looked almost lonely in the room.

"You girls start the water now," said Ellie's father. "As soon as I bring a blanket, help her undress and wrap her up, until the water's good and warm." He set Ellie down on the bath mat and went to fetch blankets.

Ellie, collapsed in an exhausted heap, pulled the overcoat more tightly about her. Alison rushed to steady her, while Keisha turned the tap on. Rusty-looking water spilled out and seemed to take forever to get warm. When Ellie's father brought the blanket, Keisha said, "We're not going to have enough hot water. Can't we do something?"

"I'll have Mother heat some," he said, and disappeared.

Downstairs, Ellie's grandmother had set about preparing a mustard plaster. Heather pretended to know what it was—at least until she had a chance to ask Megan.

"It's this stuff people used to use when they were sick," whispered Megan as soon as Ellie's grandmother left the kitchen for a moment. " My mom said her grandmother used to mix up powdered mustard, flour, and water, put it on a rag, and stick it on her chest. It's supposed to loosen congestion."

Heather wrinkled her nose. The stuff smelled as bad as it looked. When Ellie's grandmother returned, she filled a pot of water and set it on top of the wood-burning stove. At the sight of her, Heather hurried to finish up with the hot-water bottles. She didn't want to be scolded for not helping.

"Need more hot water," Ellie's grandmother announced. "That old boiler's giving us trouble again." She snapped her fingers for the girls to ready and lug more pots to the stove.

Megan huffed with the effort. "I wonder what's going on upstairs," she whispered to Heather. "Do you think Ellie recognizes Ali and Keisha?"

"How *could* she? If you're right about what year this is, then we aren't even born yet!" Heather giggled nervously.

Ellie's father, who had changed into dry clothing as formal-looking as the gray suit, came down to check on their progress. "Margaret is warming blankets on the radiators," he reported. "Ellie's bundled up tight, but she's still shaking like a leaf."

He kept testing the water with his finger and at last hauled the first pot away.

"As soon as these are ready, we'll let you know," Megan called after him.

When Keisha heard a knock on the bathroom door, she jumped up to open it. Ellie's father poured steaming water into the partially filled tub, and Keisha whispered to him, "She's so pale and weak."

He nodded gravely. "Chilled to the bone, no doubt. Has she said anything about the accident or—"

"Not a word. She hasn't even looked at us."

"I'll send the missus in. And we'll bring more hot water soon."

After he left, Keisha turned to Alison. "How's she doing, Ali?"

Alison, seated on the floor next to the swaddled, shivering Ellie, had been vigorously rubbing the girl's arms. But now, she simply shrugged.

"Do you think she knows us?" Keisha whispered. "Ellie? Do you—"

The girl raised her head slightly.

"Your bath is ready," said Alison, not quite sure why she'd cut off the question she knew Keisha wanted to ask. "Come on. Let's get you in."

The blanket fell away as Alison and Keisha eased the girl up. Ellie took mincing steps toward the tub, then stepped in quickly and slid down until the water lapped about her shoulders. Leaning her head back, she sighed and finally looked up at Alison and Keisha, offering a thin smile.

Keisha's breath caught in her throat. She nudged Alison. Did she notice, too, that Ellie's eyes were as blue as the heart of a flame?

Chapter Seven

THE GIFT

Heather and Megan heated several more pots of water before Ellie's mother finally hustled her daughter out of the bathtub and into bed. "Why don't you girls go downstairs and rest for a spell?" she suggested, though she herself looked weary, too. "You've been just wonderful through all this, but, you were expecting a party."

"No, we—"

Alison cut Keisha off with an elbow in the ribs.

"That cider's probably cold by now, but you're welcome to it," added Ellie's mother. "And the cookies are fresh."

"Thank you," Megan said for them all. "We'll be in the living room if you need us again." She couldn't wait to tell the others the plan that had been hatching in the back of her brain.

Their party shoes clattered on the bare stairs, through the kitchen, then down the hall. How naked and forlorn the Christmas tree looked in the great room! On the floor beneath it, boxes of fragile, glistening red, green, and silver balls and tinsel were heaped alongside strings of lights, popcorn and cranberries, and tiny beads. At the sight of a delicate Victorian angel ornament, Megan drew her breath in sharply. Her heart beat fast as she fingered the white lace and seed-pearl trim.

"Do you think she's going to be okay?" asked Heather with a mouthful of iced butter cookie.

"If she's anything like her grandma, she will be," said Keisha, and everyone laughed.

Megan touched the piano keys tentatively, wishing she could play. What Ellie and her family needed was a little Christmas spirit. She cleared her throat to get the other girls' attention. "I feel kind of sorry for Ellie, don't you?" The others nodded and she pressed on. "Maybe we can cheer her up a little."

As the girls set about preparing their surprise, Keisha burst into "Deck the Halls." Alison and Megan joined in.

"Come on, Heather, sing." said Alison. "Don't be a party pooper."

"I—I'm not trying to be," Heather stammered. "I just—"

"Can't remember all the words?" Alison gave her a lopsided grin.

"Never knew 'em," Heather mumbled. When her friends raised their eyebrows, she added, "It's not exactly a traditional Chanukah song."

Keisha giggled. "I guess not! No wonder you didn't have an ornament."

"Why didn't you just say you're Jewish?" asked Alison.

"Well, it never came up until now." Heather shrugged. "It's not like it's a secret or anything. Sometimes it's hard, though, being different."

"We're *all* different," teased Megan, waving the ends of her reddish-blond hair as a reminder, "in case you didn't notice."

"She's right," Keisha chimed in. "Different strokes for different folks. We celebrate Kwanzaa. It's a Swahili word that means 'the first fruits of harvest.' We practice a special principle each day for seven days. Every night for a week we light a new candle, pretty much the way Jewish families do."

"What's *your* candleholder called?" asked Heather.

"Kinara."

"Sounds kind of like menorah, doesn't it?" Heather grinned at the similarity, then pulled the others into a huddle.

Ten minutes later, the girls were hurrying up the stairs.

"I can't wait to see her face," said Keisha.

"Me either." Alison wondered whether the others had noticed Ellie's eyes. Did they, too, have the feeling they'd seen them somewhere before?

Heather, Keisha, and Alison burst into Ellie's room. Ellie was swaddled so tightly, they could see nothing but her pale face on the pillow. Her parents were seated side by side at the foot of the narrow bed, holding hands. Her grandmother was fussing over her, trying to get her to swallow a spoonful of something that smelled strongly of camphor. A small blue jar sat uncapped on the nightstand.

Keisha, standing closest, sniffed, then caught the

startled woman's hand. "You shouldn't do that. It's bad for her. My mom says you're only supposed to put that stuff on your chest."

"Mrs. Vance knows these things," Alison confirmed. "She's a nurse." Though Ellie's grandmother looked unconvinced, Ellie herself offered a thin smile of gratitude.

"Really," said Keisha. "My bottle even says 'Not to be taken internally.'"

"Mother, please." Ellie's father motioned for the woman to put the spoon down. He looked grateful for the information. "We all want what's best here."

When Ellie's grandmother gave in, Heather said, "Well?"

Holding out their brimming skirts, Alison and Keisha passed among Ellie's family with candelabras and candles from downstairs, urging them to fill the holders and light the candles. Heather sat down beside Ellie, revealing a lap full of tinsel, garlands, and a few of the less breakable ornaments. She helped free Ellie's hands from the blankets and gave her the decorations. Ellie frowned but said nothing. On Keisha's downbeat, Alison and

Keisha began singing "O, Tannenbaum." Heather hummed along, and the family quickly joined in.

Right on cue, Megan entered the room. Fragrant spruce boughs were tied about her waist and shoulders. The golden stars on her dress peeked through necklaces of popcorn and cranberries and tiny glass beads. Megan the Human Christmas Tree!

Keisha managed to keep singing, barely, but Alison and Heather had no such luck; they were giggling too much. Ellie's grandmother clapped her hands with delight as the adults launched into the next verse with new vigor. Ellie herself was grinning so hard that her cheeks looked like little rosy apples. At the end of the song, everyone shouted, "Merry Christmas!"

Megan squeezed past the others, stepping close enough for Ellie to hang a couple of ornaments and to toss tinsel on her branches. Then she handed her the exquisite Victorian angel. "For the top," she said, bending forward. She tried hard to keep a straight face while Ellie set it on her head.

"What you've done, it's like magic!" Ellie whispered. She glanced around and smiled. Flames and their mirrored reflections danced about the crowded room, flickering on all the joyous faces. And Ellie's flame-blue eyes outshone them all.

C h a p t e r
Eight

THE MAGIC ATTIC CLUB

T he grandfather clock bonged downstairs. Alison found herself counting the strokes. Was it that late already? She nudged Heather and Keisha. "We'd better go," she whispered, then turned to Ellie and her family. "It's late," she said. "Our folks are expecting us."

Ellie's parents rose and hugged each girl in turn, thanking them for coming and for saving the party. Ellie's grandmother added a wave and holiday wishes.

Ellie squeezed their hands and smiled. "I'll be fine,"

she said. "Thank you all—for everything."

"You take care, okay?" Megan handed the angel to Ellie. "We'll see you later."

"I'll show you out," said Ellie's father.

"Oh, no." Alison replied quickly. "Stay with your family. We know the way." Under her breath she added, "I hope."

They waved good-bye, then slipped out into the hall and closed the door. At the head of the stairs, Alison stopped short. "Where are we going?" she whispered. "There aren't any other houses out there. We saw that before."

The girls stared at each other, realizing that they'd been so wrapped up in helping Ellie that they'd forgotten they had no idea where they actually were.

"Now what?" Heather bit her lip.

Megan caught a glimpse of the mirror in the room they'd first entered. She waved the others inside and shut the door. Only the candle on the windowsill lit the room.

The girls wondered whether they shared the same thought. Why not try the mirror again? What did they have to lose?

Heather shivered. "Do you really think it will work?" she asked, as she and the others stripped the boughs and garlands off Megan.

"We won't know until we try," Keisha said.

They stood before the mirror. Megan stared at their reflections and thought of all the questions she was bursting to ask Ms. Eleanor Goodwin when they got back—*if* they got back. In the darkening room, the girls had to strain to see anything at all. Holding hands, they closed their eyes.

A heartbeat later, daylight stabbed their eyes. Ms. Goodwin's attic spread before them like welcoming arms.

"We're back!" Megan exclaimed in wonder.

"Are you sure we really went?" Alison frowned, hardly able to believe what had just happened. "I mean, the whole thing was incredible. . . . And *you*!" She pointed at Megan and giggled. "A walking, talking Christmas tree!"

"Aha!" cried Keisha, reaching over and plucking something from Megan's hair. "The proof is in the popcorn."

The girls laughed. "Come on," said Heather. "Let's change our clothes. I'm absolutely dying to talk to Ms. Goodwin."

"Yes," Megan said, with a knowing smile at the others, "me, too."

Once the dresses were stored away, Megan relocked the attic and the girls hurried to the sitting room. They found Ms. Goodwin reading on the sofa with the white terrier snuggled in the crook of one arm.

"Why, there you are!" Ms. Goodwin's face seemed to come alive at the sight of the girls. "Did you enjoy yourselves?"

"We had the most amazing adventure," said Keisha. "You should have been there."

Heather locked eyes with Megan and said, "Maybe she was." Ms. Goodwin winked at the girls. Alison and Keisha exchanged unspoken words of their own.

"But how does it work?" asked Alison, dancing in place.

"Exactly where were we? Can we do it again? Don't leave anything out." Megan sat expectantly at Ms. Goodwin's feet. Heather and the others did, too.

"Is it the mirror?" asked Keisha, breathless.

"Of course," Ms. Goodwin confided. "But the *real* magic is in you."

Alison looked unconvinced. "But what do we *do*?"

Ms. Goodwin smiled. "First, take the key. You know where it is now." She gestured toward the silver box in the entry hall, and Megan jumped up to return the key. "And you're always welcome to use it. Then, all you need to do is choose a costume and look into the mirror."

"Do we always come and go through the same one?" Keisha asked.

"Yes and no." Ms. Goodwin laughed at the girls' confused expressions. "You always go through that mirror in the attic. But after you've lived your adventure, any mirror will take you home."

"You told us you and your friends used to play in the attic," Alison said. "Did you—"

"*Mais oui!* All the time. I've always loved to travel. Remind me to tell you about the camel I rode to the Great Pyramids, or the time we went looking for the Loch Ness monster."

The girls squirmed with excitement, thinking of all the places Ms. Goodwin had been, of the stories she could tell them.

"I hope someday I can travel for a living." Megan sighed wistfully. If she weren't a foreign correspondent like her father, maybe she'd be a pilot like Heather's, or an archaeologist.

"And perhaps you shall," Ms. Goodwin said.

"Hey!" exclaimed Keisha, her eyes gleaming. "Let's start a club!"

"Why, that's just what *we* did," said Ms. Goodwin. "The Attic Angels, we called ourselves. But I'm sure you can come up with something fresh, something all your own."

The girls talked among themselves for a few minutes, and Heather cried, "I've got it! The Magic Attic Club! How about that? Or maybe—"

"No, that's perfect," said Alison, and the others nodded enthusiastically.

"If you want," Megan said, "we could have an official notebook or something and write up stuff about our adventures."

"And the only rule," Alison suggested, "is that we have to promise to tell one another everything if we go through the mirror alone."

"Cool." Keisha grinned. "Ms. Goodwin, what do you think?"

"Well, first off, I think you should call me Ellie, if you don't mind. It's not nearly so formal."

The girls broke into wide grins. Heather answered for them all: "Ellie it is!"

"Splendid! And as for the Magic Attic Club, well, I think it's a simply marvelous name!" Ms. Goodwin rubbed Monty's ear and gazed fondly about the room.

"My, it's good to be home. And just in time."

Heather and Megan exchanged a look of confusion. "For Christmas, you mean?" asked Megan. "But you don't even have a tree."

"Yes I do, dear. It's in the living room."

"How have you even had time to unpack?" Heather frowned. "Whenever *we* move—"

"Oh, but you must understand, this is my family home—as you've probably guessed—and most everything stays right here, waiting for me, when I'm abroad performing and visiting old friends."

"But what about the van?" asked Alison.

"Oh, that." Ellie dismissed the question with a flip of her scarf. "There are quite simply *some* things I can't be without. Not for years at a time, at any rate. And my caretaker saw to the tree."

"Why not let us decorate it with you?" said Heather. The others nodded eagerly. "We can string popcorn and cranberries like in the olden days." The girls couldn't help grinning at Megan—and Ellie smiled, too.

"Hey," Alison said, "maybe you guys can bring your menorah and kinara—just for awhile. What do you think? It'll be great!"

"Brava!" Ellie said, clapping her hands. "I'll put some mulled cider on and boil up a batch of taffy. And while it's cooling, we can trim the tree. How does that sound?"

No one answered. All eyes were on Heather.

"Like fun. Absolutely! We can even sing "Deck the Halls." I'm a pro on the chorus," Heather chimed in.

The whole Magic Attic Club laughed as one. Ellie rose gracefully from the sofa. "Well, you'd best run along now and tell your mothers our plans, while I get to work in the kitchen."

Alison opened the door and the girls stepped into the afternoon cold. Snow drifted to the ground like goosedown from a gigantic feather bed. The path would need shoveling for sure.

"What about sledding?" asked Heather.

Keisha waved away her concern. "We can do that any time."

Megan sighed. "This is the best Christmas Eve day I've ever spent."

"Me, too." Alison linked arms with Megan.

Heather and Keisha exchanged a grin. "Me three," said Keisha, hitching on.

"Me four," Heather joined in.

The girls stopped at the picket fence, and Heather suggested that they each return with something for the party. She'd bring a menorah, and Keisha would supply a kinara. Megan volunteered to provide some of her favorite

icicle ornaments, and Alison had already set aside some of her mother's gourmet cookies for their original party.

Megan, who had the farthest to go, hurried away. Giddy and still dreamy from their adventure, her cheeks flushed at the mere idea of all the places she'd go for real, not just in books. Could she really be that brave?

Alison and Keisha turned left. Alison couldn't help wondering whether Ellie's attic adventures might help her discover new things about herself. Would she be a famous athlete?

Keisha, too, kept her thoughts to herself, though she smiled when she pictured the family tree she was compiling. Maybe she could go through the mirror and meet her ancestors. Wouldn't it be great to talk to them, to have them somehow be a real part of her life?

Heather crossed the street, her mind spinning. Her father had promised no more moves. And now, with the Magic Attic Club, she was happier than ever to stay. Finally, she had a holiday to share with *friends*. But what if her father were transferred again? She pushed the worry from her mind.

Glancing back at the gabled attic over Ellie's front parlor, Heather wriggled with excitement at the thought of going up there again. In the front window stood the tree, dark and bare behind the lacy curtains.

Suddenly, the hanging panels moved, just as they had earlier in the day. But this time Heather laughed out loud. It was only Monty, she realized, playing in the folds.